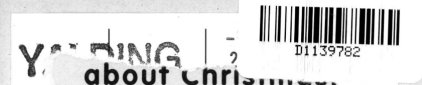

about Christmas!

"Good afternoon everybody and welcome!"
Daisy's headmaster

☆

"Oh no."
Daisy's teacher

☆

"Look out!"
Daisy's mum

☆

"Baaaaaaaaaaaaaaaaaaaaaa CRASH!"
The Woolly Wonkas

☆

"Oops!"
Daisy

☆

"Gulp."
Gabby

DAISY

and the TROUBLE with
CHRISTMAS

by Kes Gray

RED FOX

DAISY AND THE TROUBLE WITH CHRISTMAS
A RED FOX BOOK 978 1 862 30497 0

First published in Great Britain by Red Fox,
an imprint of Random House Children's Books
A Random House Group Company

This edition published 2009

1 3 5 7 9 10 8 6 4 2

Set in Vag Rounded

Red Fox Books are published by Random House Children's Books,
61–63 Uxbridge Road, London W5 5SA

www.daisyclub.co.uk

Addresses for companies within The Random House Group Limited
can be found at: www.randomhouse.co.uk/offices.htm

THE RANDOM HOUSE GROUP Limited Reg. No. 954009

A CIP catalogue record for this book is available from the British Library.

Printed and bound in Great Britain by
CPI Bookmarque, Croydon, CR0 4TD

To Santa

CHAPTER 1

The **trouble with Christmas** is it's
tOOOOOOOOOOOOOOOOOOOOOOOO
OOOOOOOOOOOOOOOOOOOOOOOO
OOOOOOOOOOOOOOOOOOOOOOOO
OOOOOOOOOOOOOOOOOOOOOOOO
OOOOOOOOOOOOOOOOOOOOOOOO
OOOOOOOOOOOOOOOOOOOOOOOO
OOOOOOOOOOOOOOOOOOOOOOOO
OOOOOOOOOOOOOOOOOOOOOOOO
OOOOOOOOOOOOOOOOOOOOOOOO
OOOOOOOOOOOOOOOOOOOOOOOO
OOOOOOOOOOOOOOOOOOOOOOOO
OOOOOOOOOOOOOOOOOOOOOOOO

OOOOOOOOOOOOOOOOOOOOOOOOOOOO
OOOOOOOOOOOOOOOOOOOOOOOOOOOO
OOOOOOOOOOOOOOOOOOOOOOOOOOOO
OOOOOOOOOOOOOOOOOOOOOOOOOOOO
OOOOOOOOOOOOOOOOOOOOOOOOOOOO
OOOOOOOOOOOOOOOOOOOOOOOOOOOO
OOOOOOOOOOOOOOOOOOOOOOOOOOOO
OOOOOOOOOOOOOOOOOOOOOOOOOOOO
OOOOOOOOOOOOOOOOOOOOOOOOOOOO
OOOOOOOOOOOOOOOOOOOOOOOOOOOO
OOOOOOOOOOOOOOOOOOOOOOOOOOOO
EXCITING!!!!!!!!!!!!!!!!!!!!!!!!!!!!!!!!!!!
!!!!!!!!!!!!

If Christmas wasn't soooooooooo ooooooooooooooooooooooooooooooo ooooooooooooooooooooooooooooooo ooooooooooooooooooooooooooooooo ooooooooooooooooooooooooooooooo ooooooooooooooooooooooooooooooo ooooooooooooooooooooooooooooooo oooooooooooooo exciting, then what happened in the school Christmas play this afternoon would never have happened in the first place.

WHICH ISN'T MY FAULT!!!!!!!!!!!!!!! !!!!!!!!!!!!!!!!!!!!!!!!!!!!!

Ask Gabby. Ask Paula Potts. Ask anyone who isn't Mrs Peters, or any of the other teachers, or my mum or

Gabby's mum and dad!

It's all Christmas's fault. Not mine. If Christmas hadn't made me get so excited, then everything would have been just fine.

Except it wasn't fine.

It was a bit embarrassing really.

CHAPTER 2

The trouble with Christmas excitement is it gets you all over.

It goes into your toes and your fingers and your elbows and your hair and your eyeballs and up your jumper. It wiggles into your brain through your ears. It gets you in your lips so you can't stop smiling. It gets you in your

legs so you can't stop skipping.

It gets you inside your tummy so your heartbeat won't stop going *bibbidy-bibbidy-bop* ALL the time. It even gets you in your eyelashes, so you can't close your eyes properly when you go to bed.

And it lasts for AGES!

My Christmas excitement started in September!

September is when all the Christmassy things come into the shops. My mum says it's a disgrace putting Christmassy things in the shops in September. My mum says that shops should only put their

Christmassy things on the shelves in about November when it's nearly Christmas, not September when it's still nearly summer.

But I think she's wrong. I think shops should get rid of all their normal things

(apart from sweets) in about January, and then have Christmassy things on their shelves until Christmas.

I LOVE Christmassy things! In fact when I'm about twenty-seven that's what I'm going to be; a Christmassy-thing shop owner! Who only sells Christmassy things!

Unless Santa gives me a job, that is.

The **trouble with Santa** is you never get to actually see him.

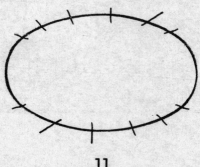

Even when he comes down the chimney with all your presents, you won't see him. That's because he magicks you asleep before he comes.

Did you know that when Santa touches the side of his nose with his finger, it makes him small enough to go up and down chimneys? It's true because I've seen it in a book. You will never ever get to see the real Santa because his magic is so good.

You can still write to him though. I wrote a letter to Santa in October. It said:

To Santa
Santa's House
The North Pole

Dear Santa,

Please when I grow up can
I be one of your helpers?
I will try not to grow up too
much because I know elves
are usually very short, but I'm
really good at wrapping presents,
plus I can bring my own red
scissors, plus I would be really
good at feeding Rudolph.
So please can I have a job
when I'm about seventeen?

Love,
Daisy

The **trouble with writing letters** to Santa is they have to be sent to the North Pole, which is the farthest away place in the world.

The **trouble with walking to the North Pole** is it will really make your postman's feet ache.

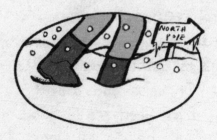

My mum says the quickest way to send a letter to Santa is to magic it there. I thought she was going to say by hovercraft or something, but she didn't. She said if I gave my letter to her on Bonfire Night, she would post it for me then.

So I did. Plus I wrote my Christmas list to Santa too!

Dear Santa,
I know it isn't even December yet, but my mum says she's going to magic my letter and my Christmas list to you on Bonfire Night. In case you didn't know, I've been really good all year. Well, nearly all year.

And when I wasn't that good,
it wasn't my fault! So please
can I have these things for
my Christmas presents:

· pogo stick that
doesn't fall over

· skateboard with engine

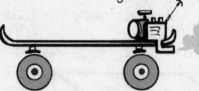

· yoyo that does tricks

· colouring pencils
that don't snap

· colouring pens
that don't
run out

· red and white football
that scores goals

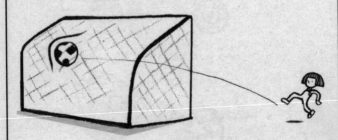

- quite a fluffy hamster

- bike that fires torpedoes

- bubble bath that makes the water green ⚡

- craft scissors with pointy ends

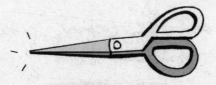

· worm house
with real worms

· big cactus

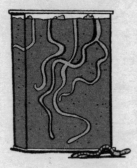 

· chocolate money (or real
money to buy chocolate money)

· skipping rope long enough for
about twenty people

· super Soaker water pistol
with about ten different action
squirts

· new watch

PS. If you run out of room
on your sleigh, can I definitely
have the bike that fires
torpedoes first?

Love,
Daisy

xxxxxxxxxxxxxxxxxxxxxxxxxxxxx

When my mum read my Christmas list, she said Santa didn't make bikes with torpedoes. Then she said that I would need to be on my very best behaviour right up to Christmas Day if I was going to get even half of the things I'd written down.

So I promised I wouldn't get into even the slightest bit of trouble.

Not before Christmas. Not during Christmas. Not even after Christmas.

I was doing really, really well – until today.

Sighhhhhh.

I do hope Santa wasn't watching the school Christmas play this afternoon.

CHAPTER 3

Before I tell you about what happened at the school Christmas play today, I must tell you what happened on Bonfire Night in November.

I love Bonfire Night, don't you?

When we went to the bonfire party, there were loads of people everywhere. Everyone had wellington boots on, and lots of people were holding sparklers! It was really exciting! (Not as exciting as Christmas though.) Plus there was the hugest bonfire in the world! It was so big,

I could feel how hot it was even when I was standing a really long way away!

That's the **trouble with bonfires** – you mustn't ever go anywhere near them because they might set you alight. Or make your wellingtons melt off.

In the field where the bonfire was I couldn't see any letter boxes at all. It was very dark because it was night time, but I was sure there was nowhere I could post my Christmas letter to Santa. But Mum said she wouldn't need a post box or a postman to post my Christmas list – she would need a man in a yellow jacket.

Men in yellow jackets are called "marshals". Their job is to let off all the fireworks on Bonfire Night, and to make sure no one gets too close to the bonfire.

Their other job is to send Christmas letters to Santa!

The marshal who my mum spoke to looked really kind. After my mum had whispered in his ear, he smiled at me and asked me for my Santa letters.

So I gave them to him.
And then guess what he did!
He put them on the bonfire!!!

At first I didn't understand. But Mum told me that bonfire magic would send all the words on my letters right up into the air, through the clouds and past the stars, all the way to Santa's home.

Just like that!

She said if I watched the bonfire carefully I would see the words from other children's Santa letters whizzing up into the sky!

And she was right! There were loads of sparks flying up from the bonfire all over the place!

I saw all the words I'd written to Santa fly right up into the sky –

Santa, reindeer, pogo stick, bike and *torpedo* – glowing really orange before they went black and disappeared. It was brilliant!

Mum said she was absolutely sure that Santa would get my Christmas letter and my Christmas list. Which made me even more excited!

All I had to do now was wait for Christmas!

CHAPTER 4

The **trouble with November** is it's got thirty days in it. If November only had one day in it, it wouldn't have gone so slowly.

I've now been waiting forty-one and a half days since Bonfire Night, but there are still nine more days to go till Christmas Day!

Oh, I do wish Christmas would hurry up!

The **trouble with waiting for Christmas** is it even makes the bits of you that don't usually get excited get really excited too!

This morning when I was getting dressed, even my school socks felt excited!

Then, when I tried on my school play costume this morning, I got excited tingles all over!

The school Christmas play happened this afternoon.

Kind of.

I couldn't wait for it to start.

Trouble is, then I couldn't wait for it to end.

Because it all went wrong.

Very wrong, actually.

Mum says things wouldn't have gone wrong at all if I hadn't got myself so excited. Gabby said that when it all went wrong, it was really funny and all my friends thought it was really funny too.

But Mrs Peters, my teacher, said

I had let myself down, my class down, the school down and everyone in the audience down too.

Oooh dear. I hope I haven't let Santa down!

And anyway, it wasn't my fault!

It was Mrs Peters' fault.

It wasn't me who told me to be in the school Christmas play today.

It was Mrs Peters.

It wasn't me who told me to carry the baby Jesus over to Mary today.

It was Mrs Peters.

And it wasn't me who told me to cradle and rock the baby Jesus before I handed him over to Mary today.

It was Mrs Peters.

So if anyone should be in for it, it shouldn't be me.

It should be MRS PETERS!

In fact it should be Mrs Peters who has to go and see the headmaster at nine o'clock tomorrow morning.

NOT ME!

CHAPTER 5

It was about three weeks ago that Mrs Peters told my class we were going to be doing a school Christmas play.

She clapped her hands after our spelling test, and said the lower school Christmas play was going to be in the afternoon, on Wednesday 16 December.

I was feeling a bit cross when she told us, because I'd just spelled poison with a P-O-Y.

And an S-E-N.

That's the **trouble with spellings**. My mum doesn't make me practise them enough.

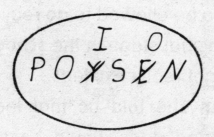

Anyway, I cheered up straight away when I heard the exciting news!

When it was last year's Christmas play, my class only sat and watched.

And clapped.

That's because we weren't old enough to be the actual people in the actual play.

But this year we were old enough and big enough and everything!

When Mrs Peters told us we were going to be allowed to do real acting on an actual stage in the school hall, we all got really excited!

When she told us that loads of mums and dads would be coming to watch us too, Fiona Tucker nearly wet herself!

That's the **trouble with Fiona Tucker**. She drinks too much fruit juice at lunch time.

Mrs Peters said that doing a Christmas play would mean lots of hard work and rehearsals. Rehearsals means practising with your teacher or your mum to make sure you're doing the acting right.

She said we would have to learn our lines and lots of new songs as well. Plus we would all have to make our own outfits!

Well, our mums would.

Then Mrs Peters said that the very next day she would be telling everyone in the class what person in the Christmas play they were going to be.

I put my hand up straight away to ask if I could be the three king with the gold, but Mrs Peters told everyone to put their hands down.

Mrs Peters said she would let everybody know who they were going to be after assembly the next morning. Then she gave us a school newsletter to take home.

When Gabby and me met my mum outside the school gates, my mum read the special Christmas newsletter and said, "How lovely! I do so love the story of Christmas! I wonder what carols you'll sing. I wonder what roles you and Gabby are going to play."

I said there weren't any rolls in the story of Christmas.

Then my mum said, "Not bread rolls, Daisy, roles roles. A role is a part; a part is the person you are going to be acting in the play."

I said I wanted to be the three king with the gold, because then I'd be rich! Gabby said she wanted to be a Mary with a blue dress, because she already had a blue dress in her wardrobe at home.

Then me and Gabby got so excited, we made up a special Christmas game to play all the way home from school.

In our game, you both take turns to think of something Christmassy that you love! The first person who can't think of a Christmassy thing that they absolutely love loses the game.

Except it's impossible to lose, because there are *so* many things at Christmas that are so loverlyloverlyloverly!!!

"I love Santa!" I said.

And Gabby said she loved Santa too!

"I love snowmen!" said Gabby.
And I said I loved snowmen too!!

Then I said I loved Christmas presents!

And Gabby said she loved Christmas presents too!!!

"I love Christmas stockings!" said Gabby.

"I love being in a Christmas school play!" I said. "Especially if I'm going to be a three king!"

But then, without even asking, my mum joined in our special Christmas game.

"I love Christmas carols!" she said.

Trouble is, then she actually started singing one too . . .

The **trouble with my mum singing Christmas carols** is she can't sing. In fact my mum sounds really weird when she sings, or even hums.

So Gabby and me had to stop playing our special Christmas game after that. We had to walk with our hands over our ears, all the way home from school.

CHAPTER 6

When I called for Gabby the next morning, my whole school uniform felt excited! Not only was I going to be acting in a school Christmas play, but Gabby's mum and dad had made Gabby's front garden into the most Christmassy front garden in the whole world!

They'd put a big dancing snowman by the wheelie bin, and a light-up Rudolph with a flashing red nose on the lawn, plus loads of other really good Christmassy things,

PLUS Christmas lights stretching right round all the windows of the whole house!!!

My mum says that Gabby's house always looks "a bit tacky" at Christmas ("tacky" means not that good), but she's definitely wrong. Gabby's Christmas garden decorations are totally brilliant. I wish I had a plastic reindeer with a flashing nose on my lawn.

And a blow-up sleigh with real sleigh-bell sounds, on my roof.

And a blow-up Santa that says *Ho-ho-ho*.

And plastic dancing elves that go *Hee-hee-hee* when you walk past them!

After I'd knocked on Gabby's door, I patted Rudolph on the head, said *Ho-ho-ho* to Santa, *Hee-hee-hee* to the elves, and then stood back on the path to look at the Christmas tree in Gabby's lounge window.

Gabby's Christmas tree is really beautiful. It's made of actual tree and it's got decorations and tinsel all over it. And it's got flashing lights. Gabby's Christmas tree lights are red and green and yellow and blue, and they do three speeds of flashing!

My mum thinks Gabby's Christmas tree lights are a bit tacky too.

But I REALLY like them!

PLUS Gabby's mum and dad leave their Christmas tree lights on all day! In my house we only have our Christmas tree lights on when it gets dark. Because my mum says we need to save on electricity.

The **trouble with saving on electricity** is Christmas lights don't look quite as good when they're switched off.

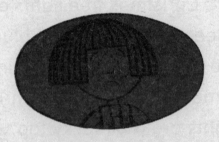

They still look quite good, but when the lights on our tree are switched on they sparkle really bright and white. Our Christmas tree lights at home look just like twinkling fairies when they are switched on. Which is just as good as coloured flashing lights.

The **trouble with our Christmas tree at home** is it's a bit wonky. That's because Mum keeps bending it when she puts it back up in the loft.

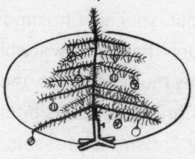

Our Christmas tree is made of green plastic, and it's got branches that you have to screw on. When it's just been screwed together, it doesn't look very good, but once we've put all the decorations on and got the lights to work, it looks really brilliant.

If I could swap Gabby's Christmas tree for my Christmas tree, I would. But I think I would probably keep my lights.

On the way to school Gabby and me played our special Christmas game again! Only this time we whispered, in case my mum heard us and started singing Christmas carols again.

"I love Christmas presents,"

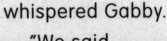

whispered Gabby.
"We said that yesterday!" I laughed.
"But I really do, though!" laughed Gabby.

"I love snow!" whispered Gabby.

"I love snow too," whispered me.

"Apart from when it goes all slushy."

"I love throwing snowballs!" said
Gabby.

"Me too!" said me.

"I love Christmas cards!" said
Gabby.

"I love Christmas decorations!"
said me.

"I love mince
pies!" said Gabby.

"I love
Christmas cake!"
said me.

"I love turkey!" said Gabby.

"I love stuffing!" said me.

"I love Christmas carols!" said my mum again!

And then *guess what*? She started singing Christmas carols again!

So we had to stop playing our special Christmas game AGAIN!

And listen to my mum all the way to the school.

I nearly didn't give her a kiss at the school gates, her singing was so terrible.

CHAPTER 7

When we got into school, everyone in the whole playground was really, really excited about being in a school Christmas play!

Colin Kettle wanted to be a shepherd, Nishta Baghwat wanted to be an angel with at least six wings, Paula Potts wanted to be a three king but didn't mind which present she brought, and Liam Chaldecott's dad said if Liam wasn't Joseph he was going to write to Mrs Peters to complain.

In assembly, Gabby and me were so excited we could only pretend to sing the songs, our voices had gone so squeaky!

Harry Bayliss fidgeted all the way through because he wanted to be a Roman soldier with an actual sword. Fiona Tucker nearly wet herself again because she was bursting to be an angel with a magic wand. And Liberty Pearce said she had done a prayer to God asking if she could have first ride on the camels.

"I sooooooo hope I'm the three king with the gold!" I said to Gabby as we walked back to our classroom.

"And I soooooooooooooooooooooooo hope I'm Mary," said Gabby.

Gabby said that Mary was the best person to be in the Christmas play by faaaaaar, because you got to wear a blue dress. (Gabby's favourite colour is blue.) Plus she said Mary can ride donkeys sideways.

I told her only circus people can ride donkeys sideways, but Gabby said she had seen a photo of Mary actually doing it. So it must be true.

I told Gabby that even if Mary could ride donkeys sideways, we weren't allowed alive donkeys in the school play, plus the three king with the gold had a camel, and camels were much better than donkeys.

Double plus, wearing a gold crown was much better than wearing a blue cloak.

And carrying a golden present was even better!

Then I said there was no way Gabby was going to be Mary anyway, because she had blonde hair.

So then Gabby got a bit cross, and kicked the wall in the corridor.

The **trouble with kicking walls in corridors** is it scuffs the toe of your school shoes.

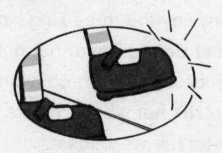

Gabby said she'd be in for it if her mum saw the scuff, because she'd only had her shoes on for two hours.

I said to spit on it when we got back to the classroom and then rub it with her finger. That always makes my scuffs go away. At least for a while.

Then Gabby said she would wear a black Mary wig if she had to, plus we weren't allowed alive camels either, and anyway the three king's present wouldn't be real gold, but her cloak would be real blue, so would her hood AND her shoes if Mrs Peters would let her wear them.

That's the **trouble with blue school shoes**. They have to be black.

Otherwise you get told off.

Especially if they're white trainers.

CHAPTER 8

When we got back to our classroom after assembly, and sat down at our desks, Mrs Peters had to clap her hands SIX TIMES before she could get everyone to be quiet. Then she had to clap AGAIN, because Jack Beechwhistle STILL wouldn't be quiet.

Then Fiona Tucker put her hand up and asked if she could go to the loo, so we had to wait even longer to find out which person in the Christmas play we were going to be.

Fiona Tucker must have been really really bursting, because she took absolutely ages to come back.

She took so long, Liberty Pearce had to go to the loo too!

Then Colin Kettle.

And then Jack Beechwhistle! (But he wasn't allowed, because he didn't really need to go.)

When everyone had come back from the loo, Mrs Peters clapped her hands two times more again, and said, "Right, children. Quiet please, children, while I read out my list. On this list are the names of the children in the class who I have chosen to

74

be the lead characters in the school Christmas play. After I have read out your name, I will read out the name of the character you are going to be. For example: Gabriella, you will be Mary."

That's the **trouble with Gabby**. She's really jammy.

Once Gabby had stopped squealing like a hamster, Mrs Peters read out all the other parts in the play.

Daniel Carrington was going to be Joseph.

Nishta Baghwat was going to be the three king with the gold.

Vicky Carrow was going to be the three king with the frankincense.

Harry Bayliss was the three king with the myrrh.

Liberty Pearce, Fiona Tucker and Jasmine Smart were all going to be angels.

Daniel McNicholl was going to be a bright shining star.

Jack Beechwhistle was going to be King Herod.

Colin Kettle, Sanjay Lapore and Bernadette Laine were all Roman soldiers, with ACTUAL SWORDS.

Liam Chaldecott was going to be the innkeeper.

Melanie Simpson was going to be a barmaid.

David Alexander, Barry Morely and Stephanie Brakespeare were going to be shepherds.

Paula Potts was going to be a sheepdog.

And all the children in the class who hadn't had their names read out were going to be part of a special gang of singing sheep, called the "Woolly Wonkas".

Oh yes . . .

And I was going to be Mary's helper.

At first, when Mrs Peters told me I was going to be Mary's helper, I didn't know what to say.

Or think.

I'd heard of a Mary before, but I'd never heard of a Mary's helper.

So then I asked Gabby what it was.

"What's a Mary's helper?" I whispered.

"It's someone who helps ME!" said Gabby, all excitedly. "Isn't it good, Daisy! You and me are going to be together on stage in the school play! Mrs Peters has put us together!

Because we're best friends! Isn't it brilliant?!"

So I forgot about being a three king, and got really excited about being a Mary's helper instead!

Gabby was going to be Mary! And I was going to be her helper! We were going to be a special Christmas team together, in the school Christmas play!

How exciting was that!

CHAPTER 9

After Mrs Peters had read out all the parts that we were going to be in the Christmas play, she made us all calm down again.

Except for Jack Beechwhistle. Jack Beechwhistle wouldn't calm down at all.

He just wouldn't stop waving his arms about and asking who King Herod was. In the end he asked so much, he had to go and stand outside the classroom door!

After about five minutes, Mrs Peters let him back in.

Then she told us the story of Christmas!

The **trouble with the story of Christmas** is it's a bit strange in the beginning if you ask me.

It goes like this:

One day (actually night) Mary (who was going to be Gabby) was asleep in bed when she had a dream.

God (who wasn't going to be anyone) spoke to Mary in her dreams and told her she was going to have a baby.

Plus he told her that the baby was going to be called Jesus, and that Jesus would be his son.

But although Jesus would be God's son, God needed a different dad to look after him. So God told Mary to ask her husband, who was called Joseph, to be Jesus' dad instead.

That's the **trouble with being God**. You are far too busy to look after babies. Even if it's *your* own baby!

Then Daniel Carrington, who was going to be Joseph, put his hand up and asked Mrs Peters a question.

He said, "Missssss, if Mary is Joseph's wife but she's having God's baby, does that mean she's been having an affair?"

Mrs Peters went a bit red, and said no, it didn't. It just meant that God "moves in mysterious ways".

Then Jack Beechwhistle started moving in mysterious ways in his school chair. So he got sent out of the classroom again.

After he was let back in, Mrs Peters told us that Joseph was really pleased when he heard the news about Baby Jesus.

Joseph was a carpenter, so I reckon he probably started carving some wooden toys for baby Jesus to play with.

Then baby Jesus started growing in Mary's tummy and everyone was really happy.

Until one day, just before Jesus was going to be born, Mary and Joseph were told that they would have to go all the way to a town called Bethlehem to put their names down on a special list.

Bethlehem was the place where

Joseph and Mary were born and the special list was an "I was born here" list called a census.

The **trouble with censuses** is if you've moved somewhere else, you have to go all the way back straight away, even if you're going to have a baby. Otherwise you won't get on the list.

So Mary and Joseph bought a donkey to take them all the way from the town they were living in, called Nazareth, to the town they were born in, called Bethlehem.

The **trouble with donkeys** is they're not big enough for two people so Joseph had to walk all the way there.

Nishta Baghwat said they should have bought a camel instead because they're bigger, plus they can fit two people on.

But the **trouble with camels** is they are very expensive, so only three kings can afford to buy them.

So it had to be a donkey.

I don't know what the donkey was called but I would have called him Buttons.

So one warm and starry night, Mary, Joseph and Buttons set off across the desert to go to Bethlehem.

The **trouble with deserts** is all the sand looks the same, which means you can get lost really easily if you're not careful. Especially in the dark.

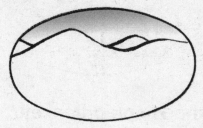

So to help Mary and Joseph find Bethlehem without getting lost, God put a great big shining star in the sky right above it.

Then some angels started telling other people to follow the star to Bethlehem too.

Some shepherds who were watching their Woolly Wonkas by night were told how special baby Jesus was going to be and where he was going to be born.

Plus three kings were told about Jesus by some other angels too.

All the kings and all the shepherds wanted to see baby Jesus being born, so off they all went to Bethlehem, with lots of sheep and presents.

Mary and Joseph got to Bethlehem first because they had a head start. Trouble is, they couldn't find anywhere to stay.

Every time they knocked at an inn, the innkeepers said they were full.

Barry Morely said the innkeepers were out of order, because they must have been able to find a space for Mary and Joseph to sleep somewhere,

even if it was on a settee. Especially if Mary was going to have a baby.

But in the end a kinder innkeeper did give Mary and Joseph somewhere to stay. He let them sleep in his stable.

The **trouble with sleeping in a stable** is it must have been really smelly.

Stables are like barns and they're full of cows and sheep and things.

Even with nice fresh straw in it, a stable would still whiff of you-know-what. Especially if a horse did a whoopsie.

But Mrs Peters said Mary and Joseph had no choice. So that is where baby Jesus was born! In a stable! With all the whiffs and whoopsies.

Paula Potts said her mum had just had a baby and if she ever had a baby too there is no way she would have it in a stable. When she had a baby she was going to have it in a nice clean hospital, and after she brought her baby home, she would give it a lovely warm cot with teddy bears in it, plus a mobile that played sleepy time tunes. PLUS she'd have a baby listening monitor and a special place for dirty nappies.

But Mrs Peters said they didn't have things like that in olden days. All Mary and Joseph had for Jesus to be born in was something called a manger. And they even had to borrow that!

The **trouble with mangers** is they aren't meant to be used for cots at all!

I mean, do you know what a manger is? It's a wooden box that you put horses' food in! You know, actual horse food, like hay and grass and sugar lumps and stuff!

There's no way you're meant to put a baby in a manger, not even if you take all the sugar lumps out first and fill it with the cleanest hay on earth. But Mary and Joseph did!

And the shepherds and the three kings let them!

If you ask me, the last thing baby Jesus needed was gold, frankincense and myrrh. He'd have been much better off with a new cot, a nice big teddy and some lovely soft blankets.

That's the **trouble with the three kings**. They went and brought the wrong presents.

After Jesus was born, all the shepherds and the sheep and the kings and probably some chickens gathered round the manger to see how special he was. He was so special everyone said he was going to grow up to be king of ALL

the kings in ALL the world!

Then, after that, everyone apart from Mary, Joseph and baby Jesus went home.

But that wasn't the end of the story, though! We thought it was, but it wasn't!

Because another king called Herod found out that Jesus had been born. And he wasn't happy about it at all!! In fact, he was even more jealous of Jesus than Santa's reindeers are of Rudolph!

Herod wanted himself to be king of all the kings, not Jesus, so do you know what he decided to do?

He was soooooooo jealous, he sent all his Roman soldiers out to find Jesus. And kill him! With actual swords!!

Then the dinner bell went.

Not in Bethlehem, because Bethlehem didn't have dinner bells.

At least stables didn't.

The dinner bell went outside our classroom door.

Mrs Peters said that we didn't have to worry about Jesus over lunch because in the Bible he would be kept safe from Herod's soldiers and he would still grow up to be king of all the kings in all the world.

Which was good, because the **trouble with trying to eat your packed lunch when you're worrying about baby Jesus** is it could make it really hard for your sandwiches to go down.

So everything was all right after that.

Until Jack Beechwhistle tried to arrest us.

CHAPTER 10

The **trouble with Jack Beechwhistle being a King Herod** is he thinks it makes him the boss of the whole playground.

Which meant after lunch he was sending Colin Kettle, Sanjay Lapore and Bernadette Laine all over the place to arrest people, because he said they were his soldiers and they had to follow his orders.

But me and Gabby said there was no way King Herod was going to arrest us. Especially if he was the same person as Jack Beechwhistle.

Colin, Bernadette and Sanjay said we had to be arrested because they were soldiers. Plus they had swords.

We said we couldn't see any swords.

So they said that's because their swords were invisible. Which wasn't true, so me and Gabby told them to go away.

Then Jack Beechwhistle came over

to us and ordered us to definitely surrender to his soldiers. So we called them all poopy heads and stuck our tongues out.

The **trouble with calling soldiers poopy heads** is then they turn their invisible swords into invisible choppers. Plus King Herod switches to cosmic power!

Cosmic power is really dangerous if it touches you, so we had to run away really fast after that!

Luckily we found the three kings with presents over by the quiet area, so we got them to come and fight with us.

Jack Beechwhistle said his three soldiers were stronger than our three kings, but Harry Bayliss said his three king crown fired golden bullets!

Then Vicky Carrow changed her frankincense into poison gas, and Nishta Baghwat made her robe into a Spider-Man net!

We arrested Herod and all his soldiers after that.

SWORD POWER!

POISON GAS POWER!

LIGHTNING POWER!

SPIDER WEB POWER!

Except Jack Beechwhistle let himself out of jail straight away, because he said he was king of nearly all the land, which meant he could change the law.

And he let his soldiers out of jail too. And gave them their invisible choppers back, which was really annoying at first, but it didn't matter in the end, because lunch time was over and we had to go back to our class.

That's the **trouble with playtime bells**. They always ring when you're having the most fun.

It was only when I was walking back to class with Gabby that I suddenly realized something really important.

I'd heard the story of Christmas, but I still didn't know what a Mary's helper had to do.

After what happened in the school play this afternoon, I wish I'd never found out.

CHAPTER 11

"What do you think Mary's helper helps Mary to do?" I asked Gabby on the way back to class.

"I'm not exactly sure," said Gabby. "Maybe you could help me get on and off my donkey sideways, or perhaps you could help me tidy up the stable so it's nicer for having a baby in."

"I'm not cleaning up the cow whoopsies!" I said. "Or sheep droppings or piggy poos! No way am I helping you do that!"

Gabby laughed and said the best

thing to do was ask Mrs Peters that afternoon.

So I did. Just after singalong time.

Mrs Peters told the class that everyone would find out exactly what they had to do in the play when rehearsals started the next day. But then she said as I had sung so nicely,

she would tell me exactly what a Mary's helper had to do.

I was so excited about finding out, it was ME that nearly wet myself this time, not Fiona Tucker!

And believe me, what I had to do was REALLY, REALLY IMPORTANT!

And REALLY, REALLY, REALLY EXCITING!!!!

Mrs Peters said having a baby was a very tiring thing to do, so once Mary had put the newborn baby Jesus in the manger, I would have to come in and help!

I would need to take the newborn baby Jesus away from Mary, wash him, bathe him and give him some clean clothes.

Mrs Peters said that when I took the baby Jesus away, the lights on the stage would go out, everything in the stable would go dark, and everyone, including the Woolly Wonkas, would sing a Christmas celebration song. (Mary and me wouldn't have to sing though, because Mary would be too busy resting and I would be too busy helping.)

Then, when the lights came back on, I would need to bring the baby Jesus back to Mary, all clean and dressed and lovely.

Plus, before I gave him back to Mary I had to cradle and rock him!

DOUBLE PLUS, you'll never guess what!

I had to say a whole line of words all by myself too!

"BEHOLD! THE KING OF KINGS IS BORN!"

I had to say ALL of that, in my really loudest voice! ALL by myself!

Do you know how many words that is that I had to learn?

SEVEN WHOLE WORDS!!!!!!! ALLLLL to myself!

PLUS PLUS PLUS!!!

I even had to remember to do a

curtsey too, before I gave baby Jesus back to Mary – I mean Gabby – I mean Mary!

Well, you can imagine, can't you! When I found out all the things Mrs Peters wanted me to learn and remember to do, I really did wet myself!

(But only a little bit, because I'd crossed my legs really tight!)

And I didn't tell anyone. Not even Gabby.

CHAPTER 12

After school finished that day, everyone ran across the playground really fast to tell their mums and dads who they were going to be, and what costumes they had to make!

Everyone was really smiley and excited. Except Liam Chaldecott's dad. When Liam told his dad he was an innkeeper and not a Joseph, his dad took him to the school office to complain.

Mum promised to make me the best Mary's helper outfit she could, but said she would definitely need Nanny's sewing machine to help her.

Gabby said if I had a blue dress, we would be matching! So Mum said she would see what she could do.

Then Gabby said it was all so exciting, we simply must play our

"I love Christmas!" game again –
all the way home from school.

And guess what? There were still
loads more lovely Christmassy things
we could think of.

Plus Mum asked if she could join
in our game too!

After we made her promise
not to sing any more Christmas
carols, we said
she could.

"I love
Christmas
crackers!"
said Gabby.

I said I loved Christmas crackers too, except the **trouble with Christmas crackers** is the toys inside them are too small.

Plus, if you pull the wrong end of the cracker off, you don't get a toy at all. Sometimes you don't get ANYTHING, or if you do, it's just a paper hat with a rubber band round it. Plus it's a paper hat that is only pretending to be a crown.

The **trouble with pretend crowns** is they're made of paper, not real crown.

If they were made of real crown like the ones a three king would wear, then they'd have real diamonds and jewels all over them! Plus they wouldn't rip if you had big hair like my Auntie Sue. Or big ears like my Uncle Clive.

"I love chocolate money!" I said. Except the **trouble with chocolate money** is you should be able to spend the wrappers.

I mean the wrappers on chocolate money look like real money, so why can't you spend them?

I wrapped the golden bits of my chocolate money around some shirt buttons once, and tried to spend them in a sweetshop. But it didn't work. The sweetshop owner said I could only buy sweets with real money.

That's the **trouble with sweet-shop owners**. They're really mean. Even at Christmas.

"I love robin redbreasts!" said Mum. (Which was much better than Christmas carols.)

"I love partridges in pear trees!" said Gabby.

The **trouble with partridges in pear trees** is I've never seen one.

I don't reckon Gabby has either. I like the sound of them, but there are never any partridges in my grampy's pear trees. Even on Christmas Days.

I've seen a blackbird in a pear tree, and a starling in a pear tree, and a sparrow and a blue tit quite near my grampy's pear trees, but I don't think there are any proper partridges anywhere near where I live.

"I love tangerines!" said Mum. Which was a bit naughty really, because it wasn't her go.

"I love party poppers!" I said.

"I love toboggans!" said Gabby.

"I love figs and dates!" said Mum, which was really naughty this time, because you weren't allowed to say two things at  once. Plus it wasn't even her game in the first place so if anyone was going to change the rules, it should have been me or Gabby, not my mum.

 "I love Christmas tinsel!" Gabby said. Then she changed it to Christmas biscuits.

The **trouble with Christmas biscuits** is in my house we're not allowed to open them until Christmas Day. Otherwise my mum says they won't be so special.

We always have a big box of special Christmas biscuits in our house every Christmas! They're much more special than normal biscuits (not including crunchy creams) because loads of them have got chocolate on, PLUS you get two whole layers of biscuits in one box!

How exciting is that! You can eat a whole great big layer, and then you can eat them all over again!

"I love nutcrackers!" said my mum. "And walnuts! And hazel nuts! And brazil nuts. And pecan nuts!"

Which was *five* things!

Which is three times worse than saying two things! So we banned her from playing after that.

So THEN she started singing Christmas carols again ON PURPOSE!

All the way home again.

Honestly. Sometimes my mum can be SOOOOOOO not grown up!

CHAPTER 13

The next three weeks at school became so exciting we hardly had time to play our special "I love Christmas" game. Plus, once rehearsals for our school Christmas play started, we hardly did any proper lessons at all! Every morning after assembly Mrs Peters would divide us up into small groups, and then she would make us practise the words we would have to say to each other.

And then after lunch we would practise all the new songs we were going to have to sing in the play.

O Little Town of Baaaaaa-thlehem was my favourite song, but I wasn't allowed to learn that one, because I wasn't in the Woolly Wonkas.

Paula Potts was allowed to learn it because she was going to be the sheepdog and "sheepdog" has the word "sheep" in it. So that's all right probably.

But no one else was. (Although me and Gabby did learn some of the words in secret! Especially Baaaaaaaaaaaaaaaaa-thlehem!!)

I was with Gabby for all my rehearsals, plus the three kings and

the shepherds joined us sometimes, to "gather round".

"Gather round" the manger is what Mrs Peters said everyone in the stable had to do once baby Jesus was born.

We didn't have a proper manger to gather round in rehearsals though, so we used a cardboard box instead.

It was quite a big box, and at first when Mrs Peters brought it into class one morning, it looked really exciting. But when I looked inside, it was EMPTY. There was no baby Jesus inside to "gather round" at all!

Then things got really exciting again.

After Mrs Peters had put the cardboard box on Gabby's desk, she clapped her hands and gave us the REALLY, REALLY brilliant news.

"Children," she said; "girls especially. This afternoon when you get home from school, I have a very special Christmas job for you all to do. After you've had your tea, or before you go to bed, I want you to look on the shelves in your bedroom, I want you to peer into your toyboxes or hunt through your toy cupboards and find me a dolly who you think might be special enough to be baby Jesus in the school Christmas play."

You can't imagine how quickly I crossed my legs after Mrs Peters said that! There was going to be a

SPECIAL dolly in the school Christmas play, and I was going to be the one who would be bathing and rocking and cradling it!

Then Mrs Peters said that if we had a special enough dolly at home we could bring it into school the next day!

I knew exactly which dolly I was going to bring in! And so did Gabby!!

And mine would be much better than Gabby's!

CHAPTER 14

The **trouble with Mrs Peters** is she's not very good at choosing baby Jesuses.

The dolly that Paula Potts brought into class the next day was really good, because it did real gurgling

Gurgle!

Gurgle!

sounds, and if you squeezed its arm it said, "I want my breakfast!"

Stephanie Brakespeare and Melanie Simpson both brought a really good dolly in too. It was called Baby Wee-Wee, and it had its own bottle filled with actual p r e t e n d milk that you could feed it. Plus it did real wees in its nappy afterwards!

I've wet my nappy!

Waaahh Wa

Vicky Carrow's dolly did real tears and chuckling.

Nishta Baghwat's did wriggling and crawling. (Except sometimes it fell over and couldn't get up again.)

Shuffle! Shuffle!

Liberty
Pearce and
Collette Simpson
both brought
in a Baby
Dribble
Bibs.

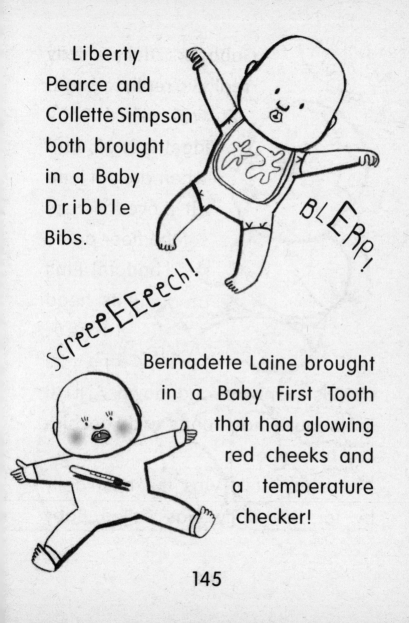

BLERP!

ScreeeEEeech!

Bernadette Laine brought
in a Baby First Tooth
that had glowing
red cheeks and
a temperature
checker!

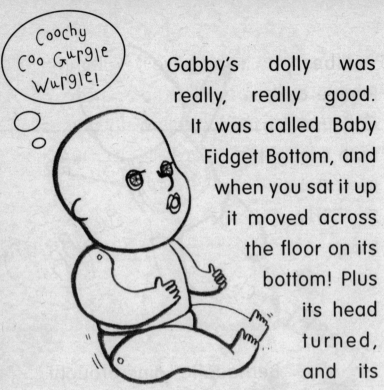

Gabby's dolly was really, really good. It was called Baby Fidget Bottom, and when you sat it up it moved across the floor on its bottom! Plus its head turned, and its eyelids went up and down AND it made gurgling sounds and coochie-coo noises too!

But my dolly was the best dolly by far. My dolly was called Baby

Hiccups, and if you gave it water in a bottle to make the hiccups go away, it did really loud swallowing noises and then went, "HIC HIC HOORAY! MY HICCUPS HAVE STOPPED!"

How good is that!

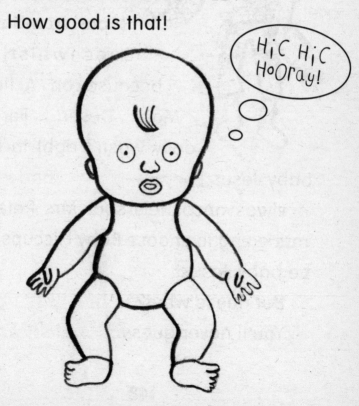

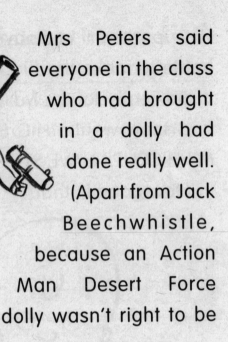

Eat bullets punk!

Mrs Peters said everyone in the class who had brought in a dolly had done really well. (Apart from Jack Beechwhistle, because an Action Man Desert Force dolly wasn't right to be baby Jesus.)

I was absolutely sure Mrs Peters was going to choose Baby Hiccups to be baby Jesus!

But guess what?

You'll never guess.

She didn't choose any of the exciting dollies at all!

She chose a really boring one!

Mrs Peters chose Laura Donnelly's dolly. And it wasn't called baby anything at all!

Laura Donnelly was really pleased, but when me and Gabby saw the dolly that Mrs Peters had chosen to be baby Jesus, we were really fed up.

After all, Gabby was the one who was going to get really tired giving birth to it, and I was the one who would have to get really busy helping her with it afterwards.

If you ask me, we were the ones

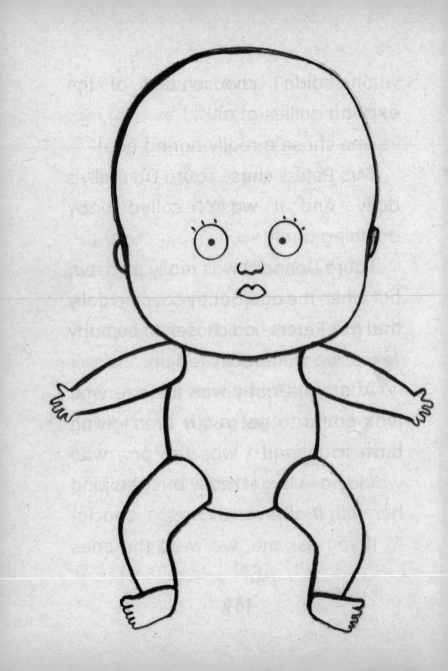

who should have chosen which dolly baby Jesus should be. Not Mrs Peters.

But Mrs Peters said that Laura Donnelly's dolly was perfect for the job.

Perfect for the job? It didn't gurgle, it didn't wee, it didn't chuckle, or crawl or fidget, or dribble or get nappy rash, and it definitely didn't get hiccups!!!

Laura Donnelly's dolly didn't have a bottle, or nappy cream, or a temperature checker! It didn't even have batteries!!!

Its eyes didn't move, its arms and legs didn't move. It wasn't special AT ALL!

WHICH WASN'T MY FAULT!!!!

When I told my mum at home time which dolly Mrs Peters had chosen to be baby Jesus, she stopped humming Christmas carols and said she was sure Mrs Peters had her reasons.

I asked my mum to go and complain to the school office about Laura Donnelly's dolly just like Liam

Chaldecott's dad had about Mrs Peters choosing the wrong Joseph.

But my mum said she wasn't the kind of parent who went into school offices complaining, even if Mrs Peters had picked the wrong dolly to be Jesus. She said being a teacher was a hard enough job as it was, without parents marching into school every day and moaning and groaning.

So I had no choice in the end.

If Laura Donnelly's dolly wasn't special, I just had to think of a way of MAKING IT SPECIAL!

CHAPTER 15

The **trouble with dollies that aren't special** is there is NO WAY they should be a baby Jesus dolly in a school Christmas play.

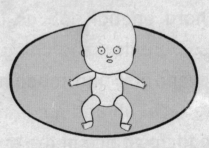

I mean, baby Jesus is the specialest most special baby in the world!

PLUS he's the son of GOD! And God is the specialest most special person in the world. (Not including Santa.)

So there was no way a plain old boring dolly should have been a really special Jesus dolly in a school Christmas play.

Especially as I was the one who had been asked to behold him up for everyone to look at.

I mean, what were all the parents in the audience going to think when I behelded him up and he didn't look even the titchiest bit special?

If you were going to be a Mary's helper, you wouldn't want to behold up a baby Jesus who didn't look properly special, would you?

If you were a Mary's helper, you wouldn't even want to "gather round" a baby Jesus who didn't do things that were properly special, would you?

I bet if Santa made a baby Jesus dolly, he would make it do all sorts of properly special things. I bet he would make it laugh and gurgle and kick its legs, and cry and wet its nappy and everything. I bet a baby Jesus dolly made by Santa would have about twenty-seven batteries in it AT LEAST!

There's no way Santa would have wanted to gather round Laura Donnelly's baby Jesus dolly. Or behold it up.

Me and Gabby tried "gathering round" Laura Donnelly's dolly every day for THREE WHOLE WEEKS, but every time we looked into the cardboard box and did our rehearsing, all it did was LIE STILL!

It didn't even blink!

Mrs Peters said that newborn baby Jesuses weren't meant to do special things, and that Jesus would do more than enough special things when he grew up.

Trouble was, I wouldn't be beholding baby Jesus up when he was grown up. I would only be beholding him up when he was just born.

So what would you have done if you were me?

You'd definitely have done what I did.

You'd have worked out a special Christmas plan to turn Laura

Donnelly's boring dolly into a really special Jesus dolly, wouldn't you?

Especially if your best friend was going to be Mary in the school Christmas play and especially if Mary wanted her baby to look much more special too.

Our first plan would definitely have worked if Mrs Peters had let us do it. Our first plan was all Gabby's idea, and it was brilliant!

Why didn't I think of it! Paula Pott's mum had an actual real live actual baby at home! Plus he was an actual baby boy!! So instead of Laura Donnelly's useless dolly, why didn't we use him in our Christmas play!

He wasn't called Jesus, he was called Eric. . .

How special and exciting would that be!

Paula Potts was sure her mum would say yes.

Trouble was, Mrs Peters said no before we even got to ask!

She said having a real live baby Jesus in the school Christmas play was completely out of the question, and she was beginning to wonder whether putting me and Gabby together in the play was such a good idea after all.

So after that Gabby and me decided we would have to come up with a different Make Baby Jesus More Special Plan instead.

And this time we decided we wouldn't tell Mrs Peters about it, or anyone else at all!

CHAPTER 16

The **trouble with taking the batteries out of your mum's torch without asking** is when she goes to use it, the light inside the torch doesn't come on.

My mum was sure I'd taken the batteries out of her torch, but I crossed my fingers behind my back and said I hadn't.

The **trouble with taking the batteries out of the TV clicker without asking** is when someone turns the telly on, the telly doesn't come on at all. Neither do any of the programmes.

Gabby's mum and dad were sure Gabby had taken the batteries out of their TV clicker, but Gabby crossed her fingers behind her back too and said she hadn't as well.

That's the **trouble with doing secret plans**. You have to cross your fingers behind your back A LOT!

At first we thought we were going to get found out about the batteries, but when our mums got some new batteries, we knew they hadn't caught us and our secret plan was still working!

Or at least the first bit of it was.

For the second part of our Make Baby Jesus More Special Plan I had to ask my mum to sew big pockets into my Mary's helper cloak.

"Why does Mary's helper need big pockets?" my mum asked.

"To fit her camel and donkey food in," I fibbed. (I'd been rehearsing that answer as well as my other words too.)

Plus I had two lots of fingers crossed behind my back this time.

And guess what! My mum believed me! She really did sew big pockets into my costume. Which meant the second bit of our plan had worked as well!

All we had to do now was smuggle our stolen batteries into school.

The **trouble with smuggling stolen batteries into school** is you need a really good place to hide them.

At first we took them into school in our lunch boxes, but Mrs Baines, the dinner lady, saw them when I was having my yoghurt and made me tell her why they were there.

I told her I had an electric lunch box

and that the batteries were keeping my sandwiches fresh.

The **trouble with fibbing to Mrs Baines** is if you're eating your yoghurt, you don't have any fingers free to cross behind your back.

So Mrs Baines didn't believe me. She said that there were no such things as electric lunch boxes, and that she would keep the batteries in her pocket until after I'd finished my lunch.

Luckily she did give them back to me, otherwise part three of our Make Baby Jesus More Special Plan wouldn't have worked at all.

After that we had to hide our batteries somewhere else.

Gabby put her batteries in her pencil case because they were smaller than mine, but I put mine in my PE bag because I had four whoppers!

CHAPTER 17

When the curtains went back on the school stage this afternoon, we were all standing in our costumes and ready to start the play.

You should have seen how good everybody's costumes looked! I was wearing a blue robe with a golden rope belt round it, and on my head I had one of my nanny's best tea towels made into a Mary's helper hat.

Gabby was really excited too, especially as she was wearing her blue shoes. She had a blue robe with a blue belt and blue shawl and a blue hairband. Plus Mrs Peters had let her wear her own hair instead of a wig!

Nishta Baghwat had a golden crown with rubies stuck to it, Harry Bayliss's three king cloak had silver milk-bottle tops all over it, Daniel Carrington had a Joseph moustache to make him look older plus a wooden hammer to make him look like a real carpenter, Liberty Pearce had angel wings made out of real white goose feathers, Fiona Tucker didn't have feathers but she had six golden wings instead, plus a massive magic wand, the Roman soldiers all had real armour made out of tin foil, plus actual swords and cardboard daggers, and the Woolly Wonkas all had white T-shirts and cotton-wool balls stuck to their balaclavas!

Plus the clapping from the audience sounded really loud!

It was SOOOOOO EXCIIIITING!!!!!!!

I was standing on the stage behind a donkey, and couldn't see very much at first. That's the **trouble with donkey's ears.**

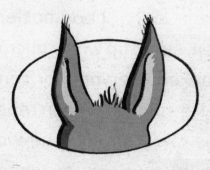

If you want to see between them you have to stand on tiptoe.

When I got up a bit higher, I could just about see my mum through the gap in between. She was sitting right in the front row of the audience next to Gabby's mum and dad. I don't think they could see us, but we still gave them a really big wave.

Once the clapping had nearly stopped, our headmaster, Mr Sturgeon, stood up with a microphone and thanked everyone for coming to see us. He said we'd been rehearsing for ages and ages and he was sure we would put on a very good Christmas show.

Then he thanked all the teachers for rehearsing us, then he thanked Mr Benedict for playing the piano, then he told everyone how to get out of the school hall if there was a fire, then he said that if mums or dads wanted to take photographs or make films of us, they weren't allowed, and then he said our school Christmas bazaar would be on Saturday, and then he said he needed more helpers to help, and then his microphone stopped working so we couldn't hear what he was saying, and then the microphone started working again, and then he said that after the play had finished, the school was collecting money for the NSPCC, and then he sat down.

That's the **trouble with headmasters**. They do go on a bit.

While everyone in the audience was clapping and thanking our headmaster for sitting down, the curtains on the stage closed, and Mrs Peters told us all to go and stand in our special places.

My special place was right over to one side, behind Daniel McNichol.

Then Miss Leames turned off all the lights in the assembly hall, and everything went dark! It went so dark everyone started giggling, because it was so exciting!

Then the angels started to sing the first song, the lights came on, the curtains opened again, and GUESS WHAT . . . Gabby had to walk onto the stage all by herself!!!!!

She wasn't shy or anything. In fact before she told everyone how poor her and Joseph were, she waved with BOTH hands to her mum and dad!

Gabby looked like a really good Mary. In fact everyone looked good. Nishta looked good, Bernadette looked good, even Jack Beechwhistle looked good!

If only baby Jesus had looked good too.

Then everything wouldn't have gone so wrong.

CHAPTER 18

The **trouble with secret winks** is you have to be careful Mrs Peters doesn't see you do them. Especially if you're doing acting in a school Christmas play.

Mrs Peters kept doing loads of normal winks every time someone remembered their words or did their acting right.

But Gabby's and my secret winks were far more secret than that.

Gabby did her first secret wink to me just after she got on her cardboard donkey to go to Baaaaaaaaa-thlehem.

Secret winks mean *Get ready to do our secret plan!* I was absolutely ready and everything!

In fact I was so so EXCITED, the tea towel on my head had started to wobble. I'd learned all my words off by heart. I'd been practising them after school, and in the bath, and even on the loo!

"BEHOLD THE KING OF KINGS IS BORN!"

That's what I was going to say, in my loudest Mary's helper voice.

I knew exactly what else I had to do too. Plus I had all the batteries in my pocket to do it!!!!!!

All I had to do now was wait for secret wink number two.

And find a better place to see Gabby.

The **trouble with big shining stars** is they stick up like donkey's ears too.

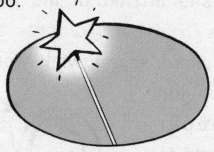

Especially if Daniel McNicholl is holding the pole and waving it in front of your face.

In the end I had to whisper to tell him to lean the pole on his other shoulder, otherwise I would miss my second secret wink.

Gabby and me had five secret

winks planned.

Gabby gave me her second wink when she arrived at the Inn with Joseph.

Our third secret wink would be when the innkeeper took them to the stable.

The fourth secret wink would be when baby Jesus was born in the manger.

And the fifth and most special secret wink would be when she handed baby Jesus to me to take away!

After that, everything would be down to me . . .

CHAPTER 19

The **trouble with waiting for secret winks** is it's worse than waiting for Christmas!

I was almost nearly wetting myself by the third secret wink.

My tea towel was almost falling off my head by the fourth secret wink.

And I was nearly fainting with excitement by the fifth one! Everything was going so well!

Everyone was remembering their lines really well, Except Daniel Carrington. He was too busy playing with his hammer.

Luckily Mrs Peters had learned to say Joseph's lines for him. Otherwise

Daniel and Gabby would never even have got to Bethlehem. They probably wouldn't even have left Nazareth.

Luckily Mrs Peters had learned absolutely everybody's lines for them, so when anyone forgot their words, she said them for them.

She didn't need to say any of my words for me though. I'd learned every single one of my seven words! Trouble is, I wouldn't actually get a chance to say them all.

I would get to say most of them.

I would get to say "BEHOLD".

And I would get to say "THE".

And I would even get to say "KING OF KINGS . . ."

But I wouldn't have time to say "IS BORN" because by the time I'd got to the "IS BORN" bit, everything in our secret Make Baby Jesus More Special Plan, started to go wrong . . .

REALLY WRONG actually.

As in REALLY, REALLY, REALLY, REALLY WRONG . . .

WHICH WASN'T MY FAULT!

CHAPTER 20

The **trouble with having to wait so long for a fifth secret wink** is my heartbeat nearly jumped out of my ears when it happened!

At first, everything in our secret plan looked like it was going to work.

I actually walked out onto the stage really well. I actually took baby

Jesus from Gabby really brilliantly. I actually cradled him in my arms really brilliantly too. I even actually managed to do a really big wink to  my mum before it all went dark on the stage and the Woolly Wonkas started to sing.

It was when I got Laura Donnelly's dolly behind the curtains that it all started to go wrong.

That was when I first realized my batteries had nowhere to go in.

That was our special plan, you see.

To put lots of new batteries into

Laura Donnelly's dolly.

Except Laura Donnelly's dolly didn't have a place for new batteries. Because Laura Donnelly's dolly had never come with batteries in the first place.

The **trouble with dollies that never came with batteries in the first place** is it's really hard to fit new batteries in.

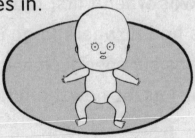

When I turned Laura Donnelly's dolly over and lifted up his clothes, I thought it would have a special place in his back where I could fit some batteries in. Or maybe in his tummy.

All the dollies that everyone else brought into class had special places for batteries. But Laura Donnelly's dolly didn't have any places like that at all.

The **trouble with not having any places like that at all** is it makes you go all hot.

Especially if you have extra big pockets in your Mary's helper outfit full of batteries that need to go in.

And double especially if the Woolly Wonkas have nearly finished singing *O Little Town of Baaaaaathlehem* and it's almost time for you to go back on stage and behold a special baby Jesus up for everyone to see.

So I panicked.

The **trouble with panicking** is it makes you do things you really shouldn't do.

Like trying to MAKE a place inside
Laura Donnelly's dolly for your
batteries to go.

At first I only pulled her dolly's
head a little bit.
But then I pulled it a bit hard.

The **trouble with pulling the head of Laura Donnelly's dolly a bit hard** is it makes it come off in your hand.

Which was handy at first, because it meant I could poke about six of my batteries into his tummy.

Trouble was, then I couldn't get the head to go back on.

Double trouble was, then the Woolly Wonkas did stop singing.

Triple trouble was, then the lights on the stage came back on and everyone was waiting for me to come back to the manger and behold the baby Jesus up!

So I tried my best.

I tried my really hardest.

I pushed as many batteries into the dolly's tummy as I could, and then I really, really, honestly tried to get his head to go back on.

But however hard I pushed, and however much I twisted, it wouldn't stay on at all.

So I had to put my hand behind his head and hold it there instead.

Trouble was, I still hadn't taken him back to Mary, and I still hadn't behelded him up.

The **trouble with beholding up a dolly with a wobbly head** is when you lift him up to say "Behold the king of kings" . . .

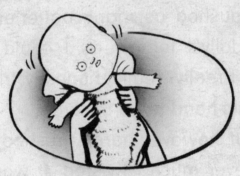

. . . the head falls out of the blanket.

The **trouble with a head falling out of a blanket** is it makes you try and catch it before it reaches the floor. Plus it makes Laura Donnelly scream really loudly.

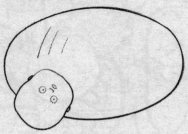

The **trouble with trying to catch a dolly's head before it reaches the floor** is it makes you drop the rest of the dolly too.

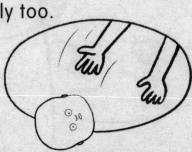

The **trouble with dropping the rest of the dolly** is the batteries fall out of his tummy and bounce across the floor.

The **trouble with batteries bouncing across the floor** is then Mary tries to help too.

The **trouble with Mary trying to help** is the batteries will make her skid. Especially if she's wearing blue shoes.

The **trouble with Mary skidding** is she will try to grab hold of the manger.

The **trouble with grabbing hold of the manger** is the manger will crash onto the floor.

The **trouble with the manger crashing to the floor** is the three kings will jump out of the way.

The **trouble with the three kings jumping out of the way** is they will come down and land on the batteries too.

The **trouble with the three kings landing on the batteries too** is it means they will skid into the shepherds.

The **trouble with skidding into the shepherds** is the shepherds will trip over the angels.

The **trouble with tripping over the angels** is the angels will crash into the Woolly Wonkas.

The **trouble with crashing into the Woolly Wonkas** is the Woolly Wonkas will charge into Mrs Peters.

The **trouble with charging into Mrs Peters** is Mrs Peters will grab hold of the stage curtains.

The **trouble with grabbing hold of the stage curtains** is then all the stage curtains will fall down.

Which makes everyone in the audience jump out of their seats. And Mrs Leames faint.

And Joseph's moustache drop off.

And the shining star snap in the middle.

Which wasn't really my plan.

But I suppose . . . was kind of actually my fault. Because I was the one who did the batteries. Not Gabby.

When Mrs Peters untangled herself from the curtains, she was so cross she couldn't speak.

Paula Potts was howling like a wolf instead of a sheepdog.

Jack Beechwhistle had gone berserk with a cardboard sword because he hadn't had the chance to set his soldiers on anyone.

And our headmaster had gone a funny purple colour all over his face.

Then, after that, the story of Christmas sort of ended.

And the story of me being told off kind of began.

CHAPTER 21

"MUUUUUMMMM!!!!"

"YES, DAISY."

"CAN I COME OUT OF MY BEDROOM YET?"

"NO, YOU CAN'T, DAISY. YOU'RE IN DISGRACE!"

Told you. I told you I was in big trouble. I bet Gabby's been sent to her bedroom too.

"MUUUUUUUUMMMMM!!!!!"

"WHAT NOW, DAISY?"

"Can we have a bonfire in the garden this evening?"

"No, we can't."

"PLEEEAAAAAAASSSSSSE,   MUM. IT'S REALLY, REALLY IMPORTANT."

"Why, Daisy? Exactly why is it really, really important?"

"NO REASON."

"No reason is no reason to have a bonfire then, is it, Daisy?"

"ER . . . I NEED TO SEND ANOTHER LETTER TO SANTA . . ."

To Santa
Santa's House
The North Pole

Dear Santa

I don't know if you saw what
happened at the school Christmas
play this afternoon, but if you
did, please don't be cross.
My mum says that you see
everything, and that if you see
children doing something wrong
then you won't bring them any
presents on Christmas Eve. My
mum says you put coal in their
stockings instead.
The trouble with coal is I don't
really like it very much. Plus we
haven't got a fire it can go on.
We've only got radiators.
Double plus what happened in
the school Christmas play today

wasn't totally really my fault.
It was only sort of really my
fault.
Mostly, it was Christmas's fault.
It was Christmas's fault for
making me SOOOOOOO
EXCITED. I've been excited since
September so that proves it's
Christmas's fault.
My mum says I always get into
trouble when I get excited.
So pleeeeease don't be cross with
me, because Christmas is the most
exciting time of the year!
Plus, if you put coal in my
stocking then you should
definitely put coal in Mrs Peters'
stocking too.
If Mrs Peters had chosen a
special dolly to be baby
Jesus instead of one with no
batteries, then Gabby and me

wouldn't have needed to have
a secret plan in the first place.
Or do secret winks.
All we were trying to do was
make our baby Jesus more
special. Because baby Jesus
is the most special baby in all
the world.
That's why I had to put
batteries in him.
Which is why I had to take
his head off.
So I could get the batteries in.
I know our secret plan didn't
work, and I know I spoiled
the Christmas play for everyone,
especially Laura Donnelly and
Jack Beechwhistle, and I suppose
Mrs Peters too, but I have been
good for the rest of the year,
Santa. (Not including the other
times I've got into trouble.)

So please, Santa, PLEASE can I have presents in my stocking on Christmas Day, and not horrible bits of coal?

I promise I won't be naughty ever again, plus I will do you a really, really good deal.

My deal is if you give me the presents that I wrote down on my Christmas list, I will come and work for you for free when I'm seventeen!

I'll bring my own red scissors, I'll wrap presents and make toys and feed ALL the reindeers, and I'll work harder than all the other elves who help you. Plus, if you want me to be more elfy, I'll even paint myself green!

I hope you like this deal, Santa. Because I really want

a bike that fires torpedoes.
I love you lots and lots
and LOTS, Santa. Christmas
is my most favourite time of
the year EVER! So pleeeeease
don't be cross with me.
Enough people are cross
with me already.
Happy Christmas. I hope
you get this letter, Santa.

Love,
Daisy

PS. Gabby says, do you make
underwater helicopters too?

DAISY'S
TROUBLE
INDEX

The trouble with . . .